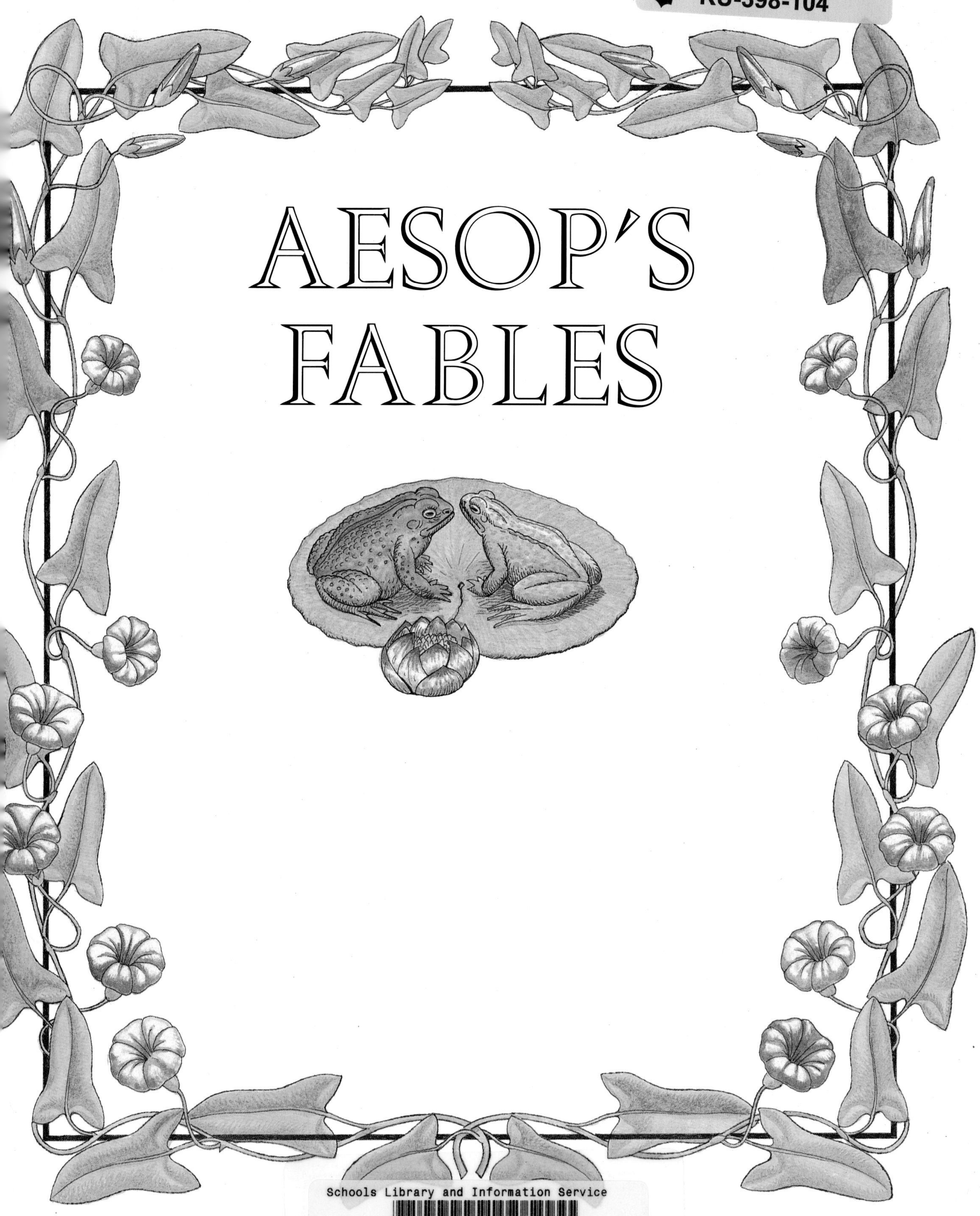

AESOP'S FABLES

AESOP'S FABLES

Retold by Jacqueline Morley

Illustrated by Giovanni Caselli

MACDONALD YOUNG BOOKS

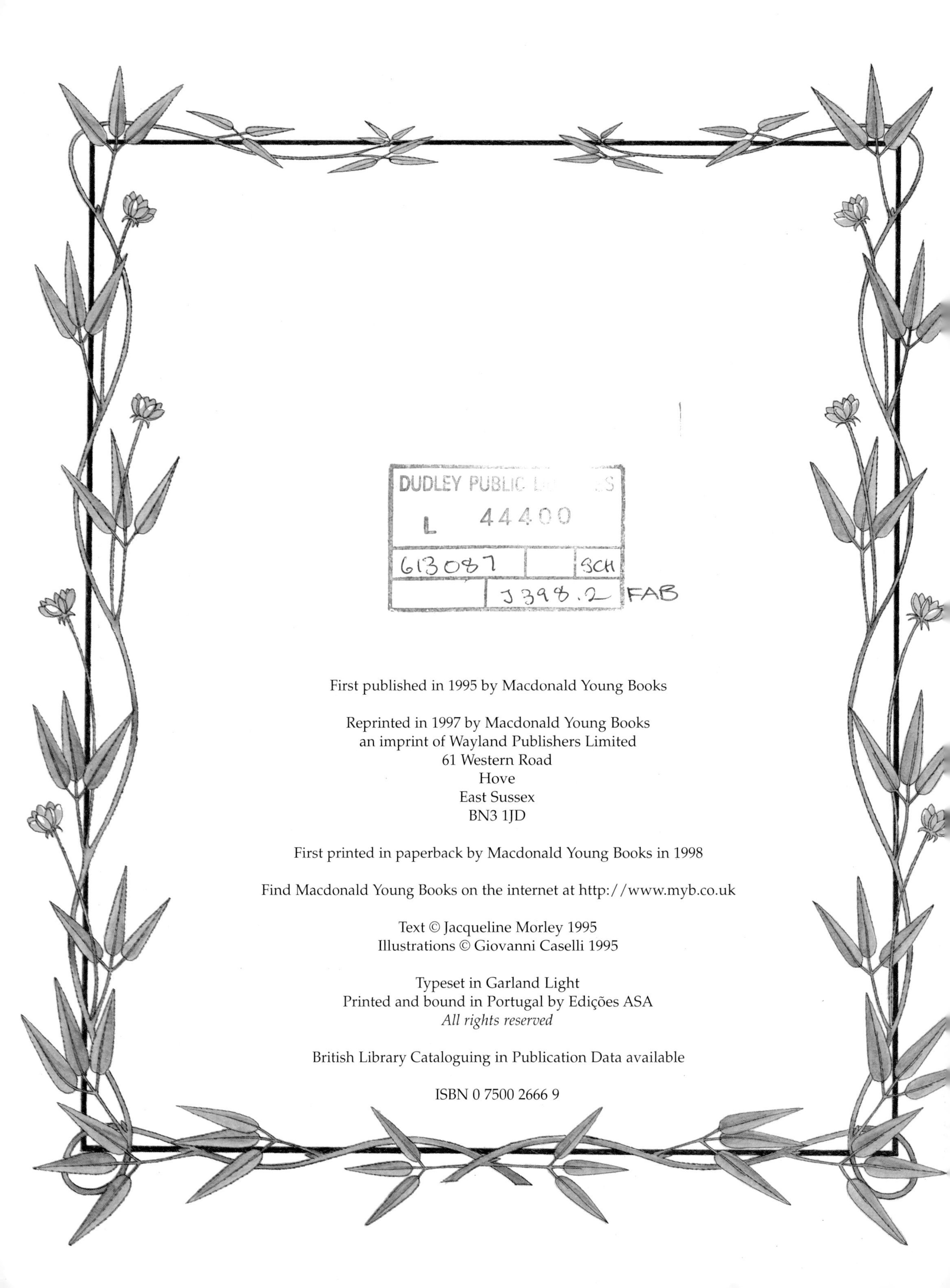

First published in 1995 by Macdonald Young Books

Reprinted in 1997 by Macdonald Young Books
an imprint of Wayland Publishers Limited
61 Western Road
Hove
East Sussex
BN3 1JD

First printed in paperback by Macdonald Young Books in 1998

Find Macdonald Young Books on the internet at http://www.myb.co.uk

Typeset in Garland Light
Printed and bound in Portugal by Edições ASA

British Library Cataloguing in Publication Data available

ISBN 0 7500 2666 9

Contents

Introduction

WHO WAS AESOP?

Aesop was a slave who told stories. He lived in ancient Greece over 2,500 years ago, some six centuries before the birth of Christ. The famous Greek historian Herodotus mentions that Aesop was a slave belonging to a man called Iadmon who lived on the island of Samos. Herodotus was writing in the fifth century BC, about a hundred years after Aesop's death, and because he assumed that his readers knew all about such a famous man as Aesop, he did not bother to record the details of his life.

This is unfortunate for us, since it means that we know very little about Aesop apart from these bald facts. But we do know that his reputation as a storyteller was so remarkable that within a few centuries of his death he had become a legendary figure, about whom all manner of unlikely tales were told. It was said that he was freed from slavery and became the adviser of Croesus, king of Lydia, the richest man in the world, and that the king sent him on diplomatic missions. It was said that on his travels he so offended the people of Delphi that they put him to death by hurling him from a rock. Some accounts say that he was horribly ugly and had a stammer, but that far from putting people off, these disadvantages only made his storytelling more spell-binding: it may be true, it may not. Others say that he was a fluent public speaker who defended clients in the law courts.

His quickwittedness was proverbial. Aristotle, the ancient Greek philosopher, recounts how Aesop defended a rich and corrupt politician by telling a story of a fox and a hedgehog. The fox had fleas which the hedgehog offered to hunt out with his snout. 'No, thank you,' replied the fox. 'These fleas are full of my blood and so they aren't very hungry. If you get rid of them, new hungry ones will come and suck me dry.' 'Similarly, if you put my client

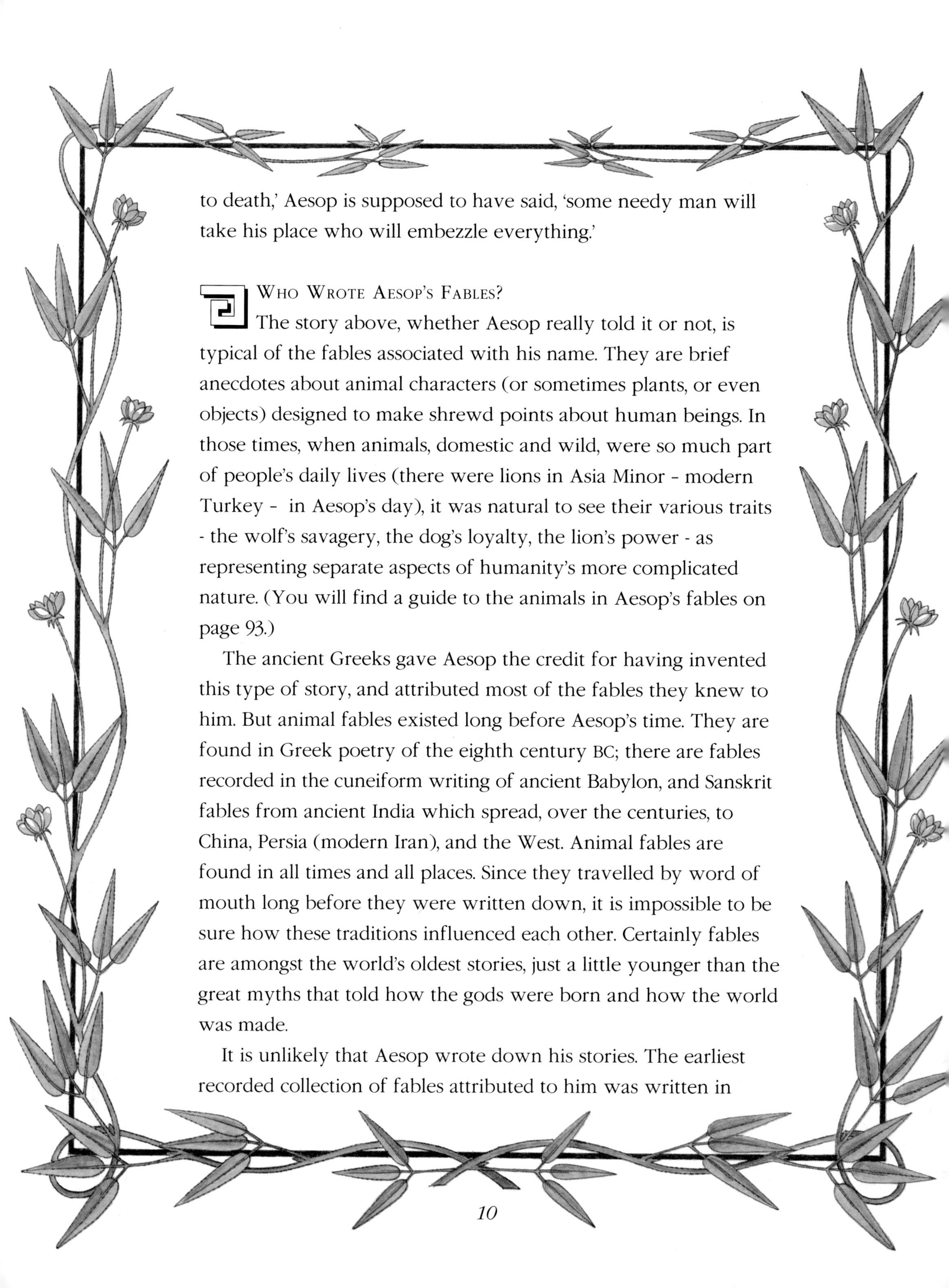

to death,' Aesop is supposed to have said, 'some needy man will take his place who will embezzle everything.'

Who Wrote Aesop's Fables?

The story above, whether Aesop really told it or not, is typical of the fables associated with his name. They are brief anecdotes about animal characters (or sometimes plants, or even objects) designed to make shrewd points about human beings. In those times, when animals, domestic and wild, were so much part of people's daily lives (there were lions in Asia Minor - modern Turkey - in Aesop's day), it was natural to see their various traits - the wolf's savagery, the dog's loyalty, the lion's power - as representing separate aspects of humanity's more complicated nature. (You will find a guide to the animals in Aesop's fables on page 93.)

The ancient Greeks gave Aesop the credit for having invented this type of story, and attributed most of the fables they knew to him. But animal fables existed long before Aesop's time. They are found in Greek poetry of the eighth century BC; there are fables recorded in the cuneiform writing of ancient Babylon, and Sanskrit fables from ancient India which spread, over the centuries, to China, Persia (modern Iran), and the West. Animal fables are found in all times and all places. Since they travelled by word of mouth long before they were written down, it is impossible to be sure how these traditions influenced each other. Certainly fables are amongst the world's oldest stories, just a little younger than the great myths that told how the gods were born and how the world was made.

It is unlikely that Aesop wrote down his stories. The earliest recorded collection of fables attributed to him was written in

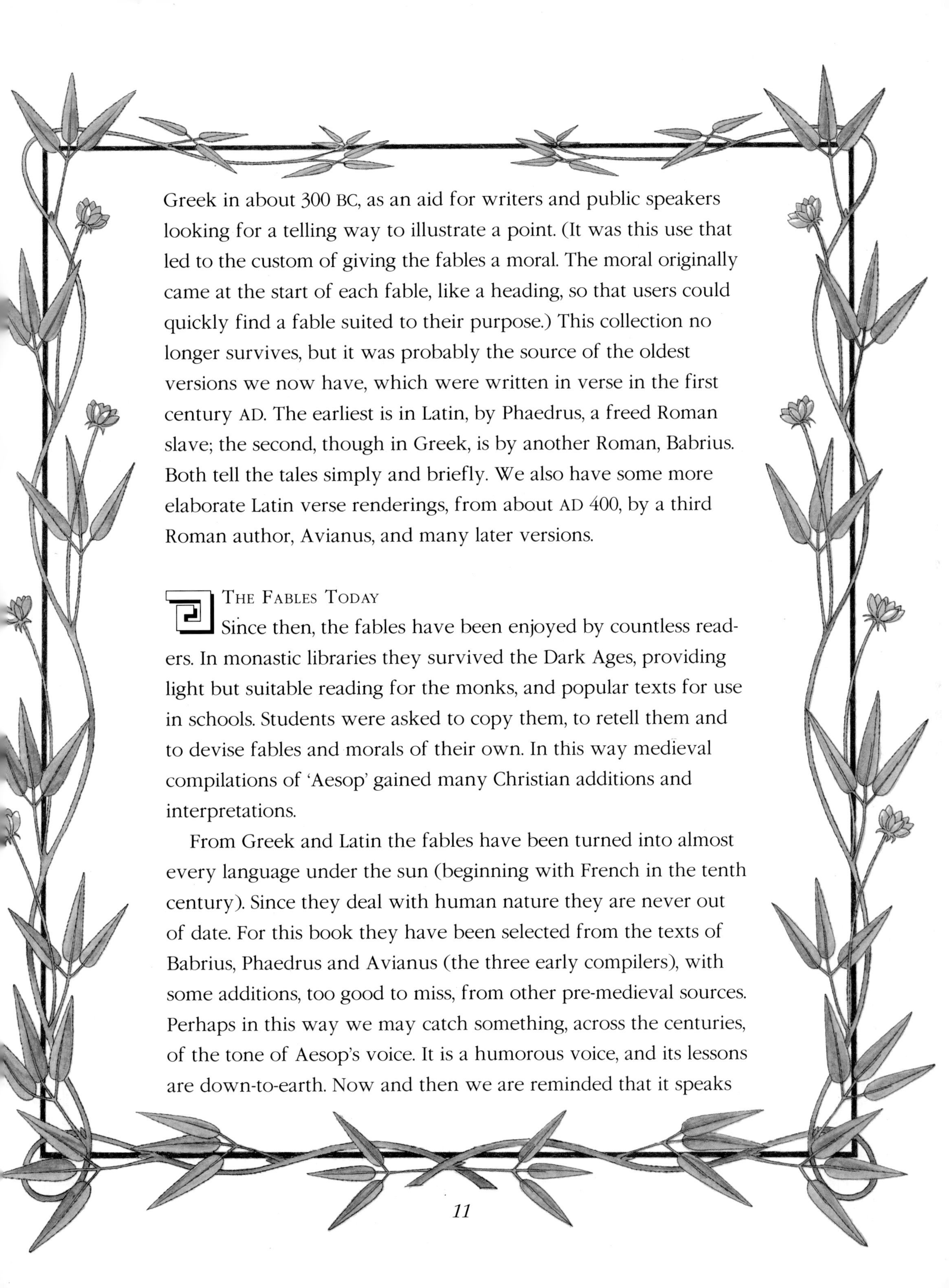

Greek in about 300 BC, as an aid for writers and public speakers looking for a telling way to illustrate a point. (It was this use that led to the custom of giving the fables a moral. The moral originally came at the start of each fable, like a heading, so that users could quickly find a fable suited to their purpose.) This collection no longer survives, but it was probably the source of the oldest versions we now have, which were written in verse in the first century AD. The earliest is in Latin, by Phaedrus, a freed Roman slave; the second, though in Greek, is by another Roman, Babrius. Both tell the tales simply and briefly. We also have some more elaborate Latin verse renderings, from about AD 400, by a third Roman author, Avianus, and many later versions.

The Fables Today

Since then, the fables have been enjoyed by countless readers. In monastic libraries they survived the Dark Ages, providing light but suitable reading for the monks, and popular texts for use in schools. Students were asked to copy them, to retell them and to devise fables and morals of their own. In this way medieval compilations of 'Aesop' gained many Christian additions and interpretations.

From Greek and Latin the fables have been turned into almost every language under the sun (beginning with French in the tenth century). Since they deal with human nature they are never out of date. For this book they have been selected from the texts of Babrius, Phaedrus and Avianus (the three early compilers), with some additions, too good to miss, from other pre-medieval sources. Perhaps in this way we may catch something, across the centuries, of the tone of Aesop's voice. It is a humorous voice, and its lessons are down-to-earth. Now and then we are reminded that it speaks

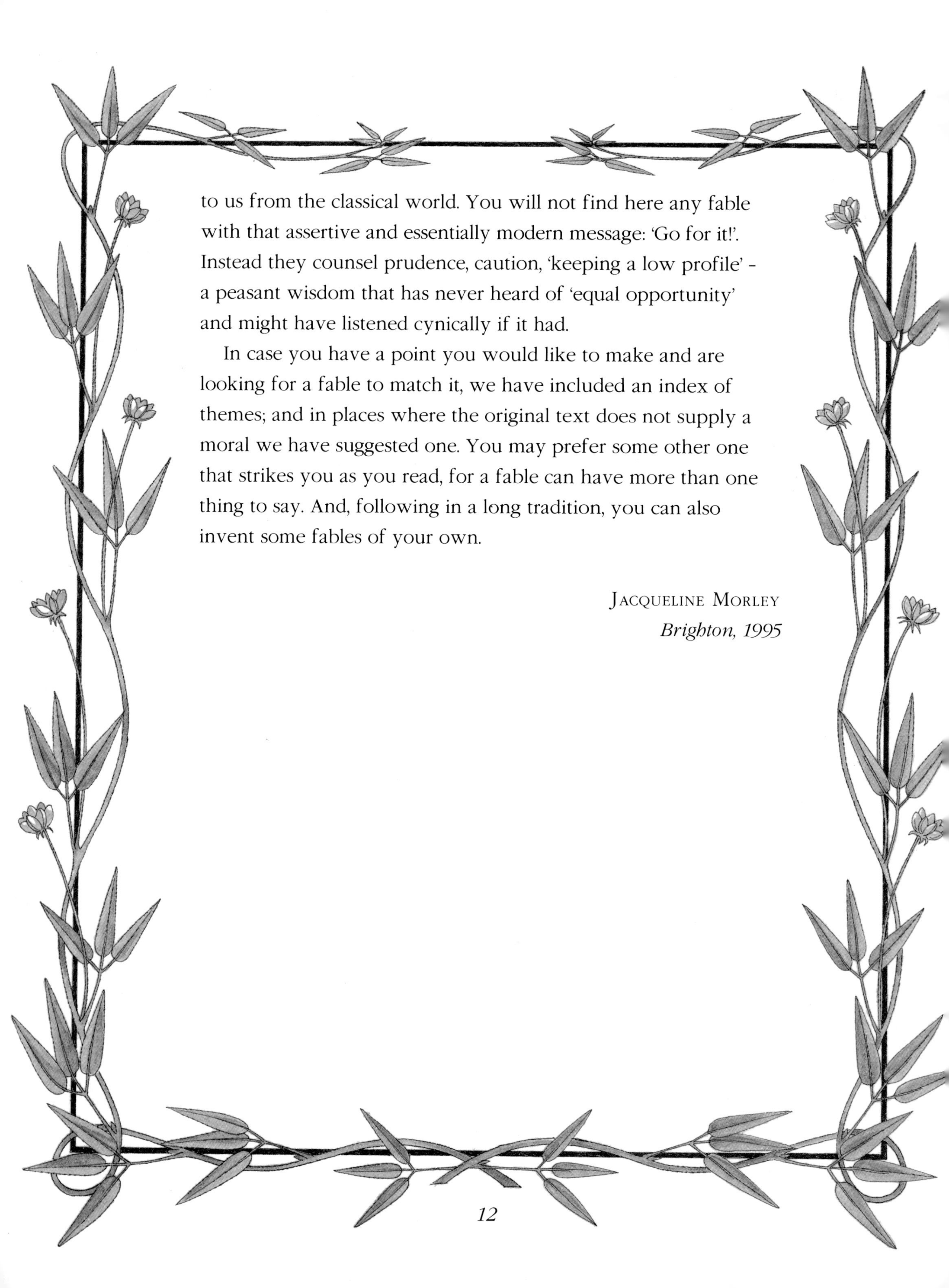

to us from the classical world. You will not find here any fable with that assertive and essentially modern message: 'Go for it!'. Instead they counsel prudence, caution, 'keeping a low profile' - a peasant wisdom that has never heard of 'equal opportunity' and might have listened cynically if it had.

In case you have a point you would like to make and are looking for a fable to match it, we have included an index of themes; and in places where the original text does not supply a moral we have suggested one. You may prefer some other one that strikes you as you read, for a fable can have more than one thing to say. And, following in a long tradition, you can also invent some fables of your own.

JACQUELINE MORLEY
Brighton, 1995

The Fox and the Grapes

A fox noticed a bunch of juicy grapes hanging from a vine some way above his head. He stood on his hind legs to get them but they were still beyond his reach. Then he began to leap in the air, again and again, snatching at the grapes with his teeth, but no matter how hard he tried he missed them. At last he realized the task was hopeless and gave up.

'I didn't want those grapes,' he said as he trotted away. 'They were sour.'

Moral

People often comfort themselves by pretending that they don't want what they can't have.

The Tortoise and the Hare

A tortoise and a hare decided to have a race. The hare set off with great bounds, his strong hind legs taking him over the ground so fast that the tortoise was left far behind. Finding that his rival was out of sight, the hare slowed down. 'What am I hurrying for?' he asked himself. 'I could walk the whole race and still be the winner.' So he settled in the warm grass for a bit, and fell asleep. While he was sleeping the tortoise plodded past him and reached the winning post.

MORAL
Concentration and steady effort bring success.

The Mosquito and the Lion

A mosquito hovered around the head of a sleepy lion and settled on his nose. 'If you think you are the most powerful of beings, before whom every creature bows and trembles, I must tell you that you are most certainly mistaken,' sang the mosquito in its whining tones. 'I am far mightier than you. Defend yourself against me if you can.'

It then began to bite the bewildered lion on his nose and everywhere around it that was free of hair. The lion clawed at his own face until the blood ran, but he could neither catch the mosquito nor make it stop. At last he had to beg for mercy. The mosquito flew off in such triumph that it failed to notice a spider's web drawn across its path. The lion-conqueror was quickly caught and eaten by the spider.

MORAL

Nothing is certain in life. Fate humbles the strong and overthrows the victorious.

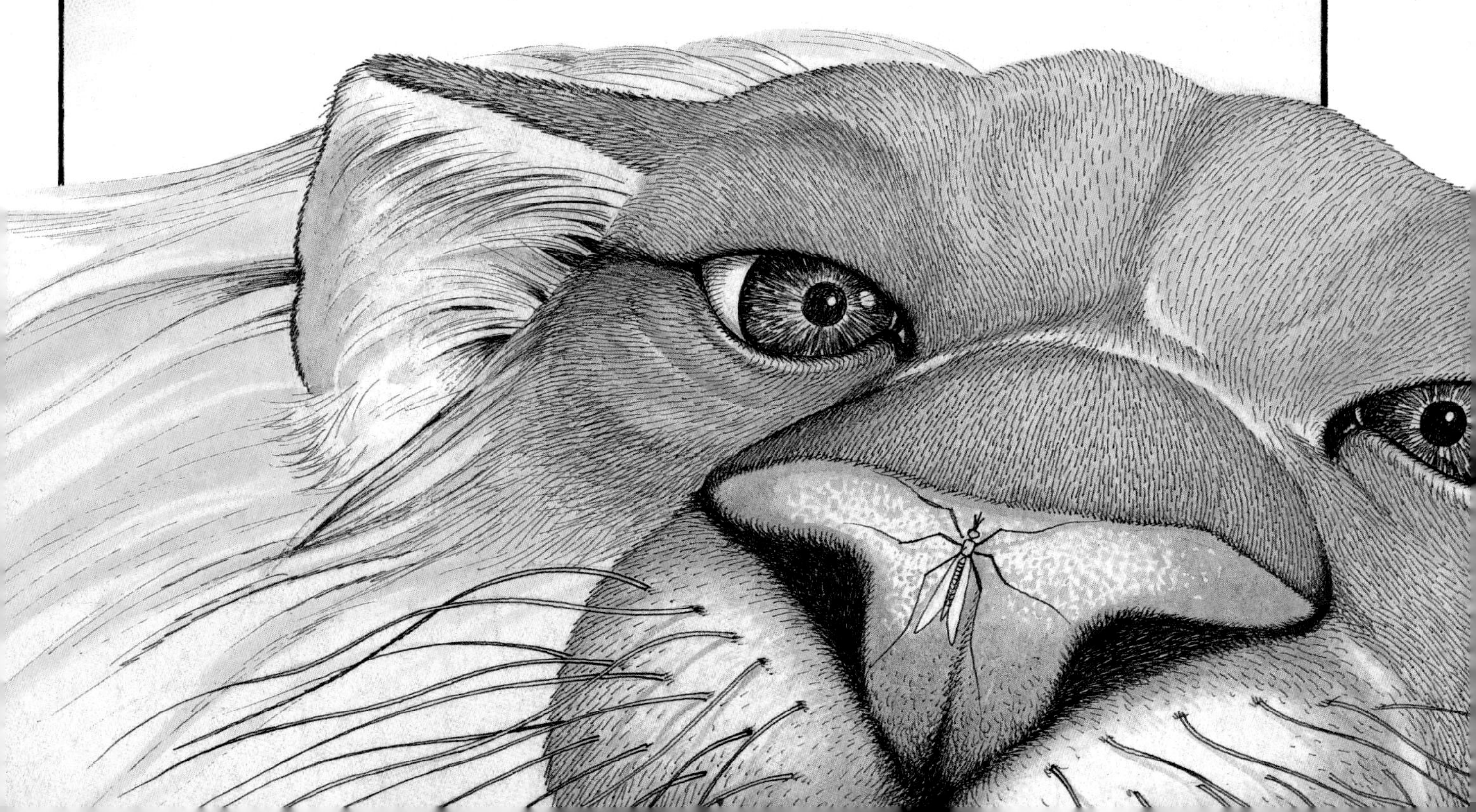

The Town Mouse and the Country Mouse

A field mouse invited a mouse from the town to stay with him in the country. The town mouse was pleased to come, but he found it uncomfortable in his friend's little hole under a hedge, and the food was always the same - nothing but seeds and damp roots covered in earth. He couldn't help feeling sorry for his host. 'You should see how we live in the town,' he said. 'Nice airy rooms and always plenty to eat. I don't have to go out and scrabble in the wet. Come and see for yourself. We could set up house together.'

So both mice made the journey back to town. They crept under the door of a house, along a passage and into a room crammed with sacks of beans, cheeses wrapped in vine leaves, jars of honey and baskets piled with figs and dates. The country mouse was astounded by this feast. They were just starting on the cheese when the cook opened the storeroom door. Both mice darted into a chink in the wall. 'You get used to this after a bit,' said the town mouse.

When all was clear they tiptoed out again, but within minutes the cook was back. This time the country mouse reached the chink even faster than his friend. 'This is no place for me,' he said. 'I'm not cut out for dangerous living. I'm going back to my quiet little hole in the country.'

MORAL
Peace of mind is better than any luxury.

The North Wind and the Sun

'You see that traveller on the road,' said the North Wind to the Sun. 'Watch me tear off his cloak.'

'I think I could take it off him quicker than you,' replied the Sun.

The North Wind began to blow and blow, but the traveller wrapped the cloak around him tighter and the Wind could not shift it.

'Let me try,' said the Sun. It came out from behind a cloud and gently warmed the land. The traveller smiled and loosened his cloak. Then, as he grew hotter with walking, he took it off.

'I win the contest,' said the Sun.

MORAL

Persuasion often gets better results than force.

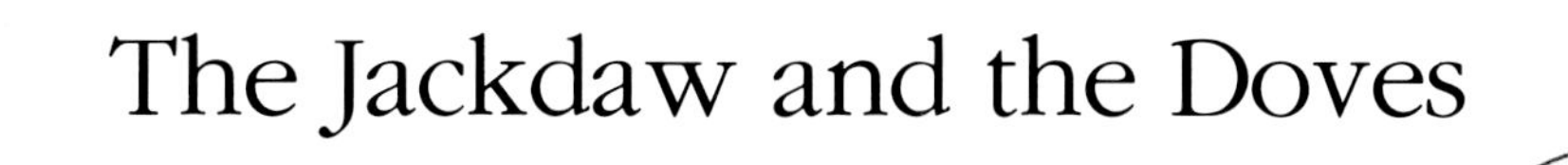

The Jackdaw and the Doves

A jackdaw saw how comfortably some doves lived in a dovecote. They were fed with grain every day and looked plump and contented. The jackdaw thought this life would suit him too and decided to join them. He dipped himself into a pail of whitewash to make his feathers white like a dove's, and flew off to the dovecote.

The doves accepted the newcomer without a second glance, and all would have been well had not the jackdaw tried to speak to one of them. His raucous jackdaw squawk startled every bird in the loft. They saw their mistake at once, rounded on him and drove him out. Dejectedly, he returned to the jackdaws, but they did not recognize this strange white bird and chased him away with angry pecks.

Moral

If you reject your own people, you run the risk of being an outsider everywhere.

The Fir Tree and the Bramble

A bramble grew at the foot of a fir tree. The fir was fond of praising itself and would often remark that it was the most important feature in the landscape, and was exceptionally tall and well-proportioned, even for a fir. 'Trees like me provide masts for the tallest ships and timbers for the finest houses,' it said.

The bramble grew tired of listening to this boasting. 'When the woodmen come with axes,' it retorted, 'you will see what good it does you to have that fine trunk. You will wish then that you were only a bramble.'

MORAL

Do not take too much pride in your own importance. It is safer to be humble and unnoticed than mighty and conspicuous.

The Huntsman and the Lion

A huntsman and a lion were journeying together. A quarrel soon arose between them over which was the more powerful, a lion or a man. 'We are the mightiest of all creatures,' said the lion, shaking his bristling mane, but the man declared that human beings were every bit as strong. 'Look,' he said, pointing to a wayside monument on which a sculptor had carved the figure of Herakles* strangling the Nemean lion. 'That shows you that men are stronger than lions.' The lion gave a lofty smile. 'If lions bothered to carve,' he said, 'you would see many sculptures of lions destroying men.'

MORAL

We all interpret facts to our own advantage - so remember that there will be another side to most stories you hear.

**Herakles (Hercules) was a legendary Greek hero, an enormously strong man of whom amazing tales were told, including one of his killing a terrible lion which had been preying upon the people of Nemea.*

The Fox and the Crow

A crow settled in a tree to enjoy a big piece of cheese he had carried off in his beak. A fox was passing underneath and saw the cheese. 'Sir Crow, what a pleasure it is to meet you!' he exclaimed. 'So many creatures have told me that you are the handsomest bird they know, and now that I see you it is clear they were not exaggerating. And they say that your voice is even finer than your feathers.'

The stupid crow was so delighted that he thought he would show off his voice. He opened his beak and dropped the cheese, which the fox immediately gobbled up.

MORAL

Do not believe flatterers. They usually hope to get something out of you.

The Hare Has an Idea

At a council meeting of all the animals, a hare got up and addressed the assembly. 'We should all live much better,' he said, 'if we shared what we had. No one would go hungry then, and no one would be afraid.'

The lions roared with laughter. 'A fine speech, hairy feet,' they said. 'But it has no teeth and no claws.'

MORAL

The rich will not share willingly with the poor, and who can make them?

or

Ideas that sound fine in theory often don't work out in practice.

The Boy Who Cried Wolf

A shepherd boy, who wanted some amusement during the long days he spent out on the hillside guarding his sheep, decided to play a joke on his neighbours. He shouted 'Wolf, wolf!' at the top of his voice, so that he was heard in the village below. The villagers left their work and ran up the hill to help him, thinking that wolves were attacking his flock. The boy laughed and thought this was a good trick.

The next day the boy decided to see if he could get the villagers up the hill again. He called 'Wolf, wolf!', and again several goodhearted people came out to see if he was in trouble.

On the third day the wolves came. The boy cried 'Wolf, wolf!', but nobody came to help him, and his sheep were destroyed.

MORAL

If you make a fuss about nothing, no one will believe you when you have real problems.

The Peacock and the Crane

A crane met a peacock who was strutting and flapping his wings. 'I can't help noticing,' said the peacock, 'that your feathers are remarkably dull. Mine are truly beautiful. Here, let me show you.' And he spread out his tail feathers in a huge fan which quivered and swayed as he walked.

'What is the use of fine feathers?' asked the crane. 'Mine may be dull, but when I spread my wings I soar into the sky and almost touch the stars. Yours scarcely lift you from the ground.'

Moral

Judge people by what they achieve, not by their outward appearance.

The Donkey in the Lion's Skin

A donkey found the skin of a lion. He put it over his head and rushed about terrifying everyone he met. 'A lion is coming,' they cried as they fled from him. But when he tried to add a lion's roar to his performance, his loud 'eeyores' proclaimed that he was really nothing but a donkey. Then all the people who had been in such a fright came running up with sticks and cudgels and beat him out of town.

MORAL

If you pretend to be what you are not, you can expect to be put to shame.

The Fisherman and the Little Fish

A fisherman, who had been fishing all day without much success, pulled in his line and found a little fish on the end. 'Throw me back,' pleaded the little fish. 'I'm not worth keeping. I'm too small to sell and there's nothing on me to cook. I'm young now, but soon I will grow into a big fish. I'll fatten myself on some juicy weed and you can catch me again when I'm really big. Then I'll fill a dinner plate.'

'Well tried, little fish,' said the fisherman as he popped him into his bag. 'It's a tempting offer, but I'm hungry now, and a small mouthful is better than none. Who knows if you'd let me catch you again?'

MORAL

Be satisfied with a small gain. If you let it go for the sake of a bigger one, you may end up with nothing.

The Frog Who Admired a Cow

A frog caught sight of a cow grazing in a meadow and was impressed by the beast's great size. She drew a deep breath and puffed out her sides to see if she could make herself as big. 'How am I doing?' she asked her children. 'Am I as big as the cow yet?'

'No, mother,' they croaked.

She swallowed more air and tried harder, till her skin was stretched tight and her goggly eyes bulged more than seemed possible. 'Who's bigger now?' she demanded.

'The cow, mother,' they replied.

Determined not to be beaten she drew in another breath - and burst.

MORAL

Don't try to be great if you are really a nobody. It could lead to disaster.

The Fox on Fire

A farmer caught a fox who had been robbing his vines, and decided to torment him. He tied a bundle of straw to his tail, set it alight, and laughed as the terrified fox ran off with his tail on fire.

But his laughter turned to cries of despair as the poor animal fled through the grain fields, setting the ripe corn ablaze. The farmer had no harvest that year.

MORAL

It may be right to be angry, but it is never right to be spiteful.

The Cock and the Cats

A cockerel, puffed up with pride, was travelling in a litter borne by cats, whom he had hired to carry him.

'I should watch out if I were you,' said a fox who saw him passing in this lordly way. 'Those cats of yours have a nasty gleam in their eye. They don't look much like porters to me. They look a lot more like a band of hunters carrying home its kill.'

When the cats grew hungry they dropped the litter, tore their master to pieces, and ate him up.

MORAL

It is dangerous to trust people who can gain from your misfortune.

The Cat Becomes a Bride

There was once a cat who fell in love with a handsome young man. She loved him so much that Aphrodite, Goddess of Love, took pity on her and turned her into a woman.

As a woman she was so lovely that everyone who saw her was bewitched. The young man asked her to be his wife. They fixed the wedding day and he invited his friends to the feast.

When all the guests were seated for the wedding banquet, a little mouse ran out across the floor. At once the bride, in all her wedding finery, leaped across the table and pounced on the mouse. Too late, she then remembered she was no longer a cat.

MORAL

A person's true nature cannot be hidden for long.

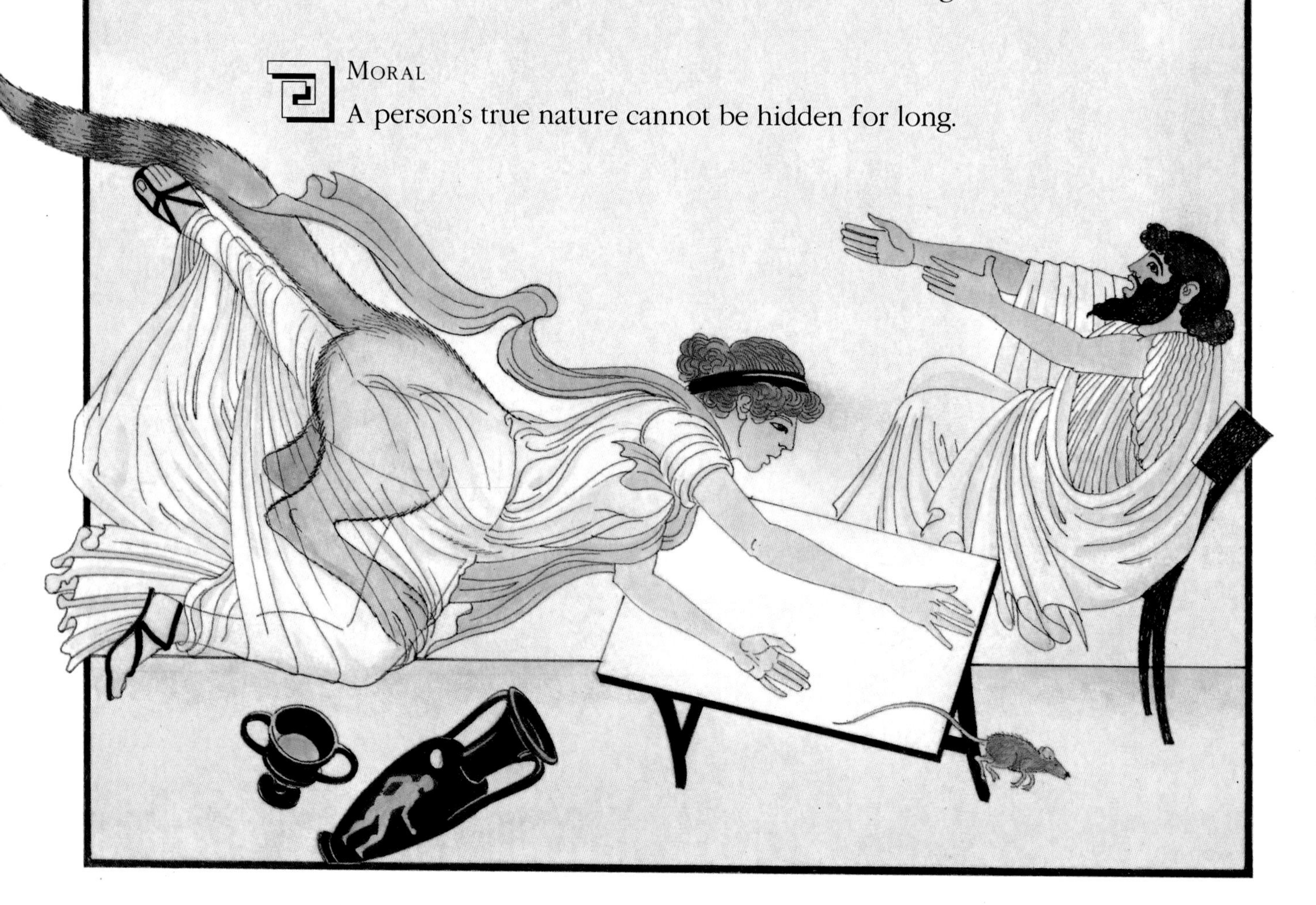

The Farmer and the Snake

A farmer's son was bitten by a snake and died. In grief and rage, the farmer decided to destroy the snake. He lay in wait for it with an axe, and when it put its head out of its hole in the rock he swung the axe at it. But the snake darted aside and the blow cut into the rock. Then, seeing that it was not easy to kill the snake and being very much afraid of it, the man suggested that the two of them should forget their enmity and let each other live in peace.

'By no means,' the snake replied. 'I can have no friendly feelings for you when I see the split in the rock, nor can you have any for me when you look on your son's grave.'

MORAL

There are some injuries it is impossible to forgive.

The Frogs at the Sun's Wedding

The Sun decided to marry, and all the creatures in the world celebrated his wedding. The frogs held a dance in the marshes and hopped for joy.

'You are fools,' said an old frog who was wiser than most. 'What have we frogs got to celebrate? The Sun dries our marshes and shrivels our ponds whenever he gets too hot. We shall suffer even more if he has children like himself.'

MORAL

Fools live in the present without considering the future.

The Four Oxen and the Lion

There were four oxen who were firm friends. They always grazed together and returned together to their stalls at night. Whenever danger threatened they defended one another. Even the lion was no match for them. If he approached, the oxen linked their horns and faced him in a line, with lowered heads and hooves that pawed the ground threateningly.

The lion saw that he would never overcome the combined strength of these massive beasts, and set about defeating them another way. He started many false rumours about the treacheries each ox was planning against the others. The oxen began to suspect each other, to quarrel, and finally to graze apart. Then the lion was able to devour them one by one.

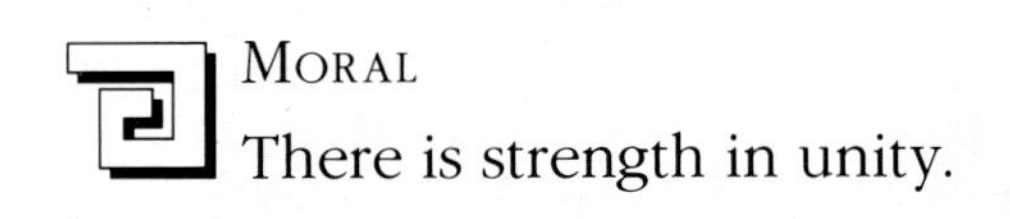

MORAL

There is strength in unity.

What the Donkey Said

An old man took his donkey to the fields to graze, all the while looking around most anxiously to right and left. Suddenly a noise of clashing swords and shouting told him that there was fighting close at hand. 'The invaders are upon us,' cried the old man. 'Run, you stupid beast. Run for your life,' and he tried to urge his donkey into a trot.

But the stubborn animal would not leave its grazing. 'Tell me,' it asked, 'will these conquerors make me carry two loads instead of one?'

'I don't suppose so,' replied the man.

'Then what does it matter to me whose slave I am,' said the donkey, 'as long as I carry only one load at a time?'

Moral

The poor have so little to thank their rulers for that one seems no worse than another to them.

The Goose that Laid the Golden Eggs

A man had a goose that laid eggs of solid gold. Every day she produced an egg, so that the man found he was rich.

After a while he grew impatient with waiting for his daily golden egg, so he seized the goose and killed her, thinking that he would find the source of the gold within her body. But he discovered that inside she was no different from any other goose, and of course she never laid another golden egg.

MORAL

Be content with what you have. If you are too greedy you may lose everything.

The Unkindest Cut of All

A woodman felled a pine tree and lopped off its branches. The pine groaned as it felt the strokes of the axe. Then the man began splitting the trunk into long timbers, by driving in wedges which he had made from the wood of the branches. 'Why did I complain about the axe?' lamented the pine tree. 'It had no reason to love me. But now these wedges, which are my own children, are tearing me apart.'

MORAL

Unkindness from those who are closest to us is the hardest to bear.

The Rivers and the Sea

The rivers got together and made a complaint about the sea. 'When we reach you, our waters are fresh and drinkable,' they said, 'yet you make us salty and unfit to drink.'

The sea was not impressed. 'If that upsets you,' it replied, 'don't come.'

MORAL

It is pointless to complain about the inevitable.

The Wolf and the Watchdog

A hungry wolf, who had been prowling through the forest in search of food, met a dog outside a farm gate. 'You seem to be doing well,' said the wolf. 'How do you keep so fat and sleek in winter time? I am stronger than you, yet I am starving.'

'I earn my keep,' said the dog. 'I bark whenever strangers come to the gate, and at night I roam about the farm to keep away thieves. In return I get a snug kennel, and food every day. The servants give me titbits too, and sometimes my master throws me a bone from his own plate. It's a fine life. Why don't you try it?'

'I will indeed,' said the wolf. 'It seems I've been a fool to live so long in the snow and rain.' So the two set off to the farmhouse together.

As they went along the wolf noticed a sore place around the dog's neck and asked what it was.

'Oh, that is the mark of the chain they use to fasten me up in the daytime. They think I'm restless, and it's true I can't help tugging on it.'

'But if you want to go somewhere, will they let you?' asked the wolf.

'Why, no,' said the dog. 'Not during the day.'

'So that is the price you pay for your fine house and food!' exclaimed the wolf, and he turned and ran back into the forest.

MORAL
Freedom is worth more than all the comforts a slave may enjoy.

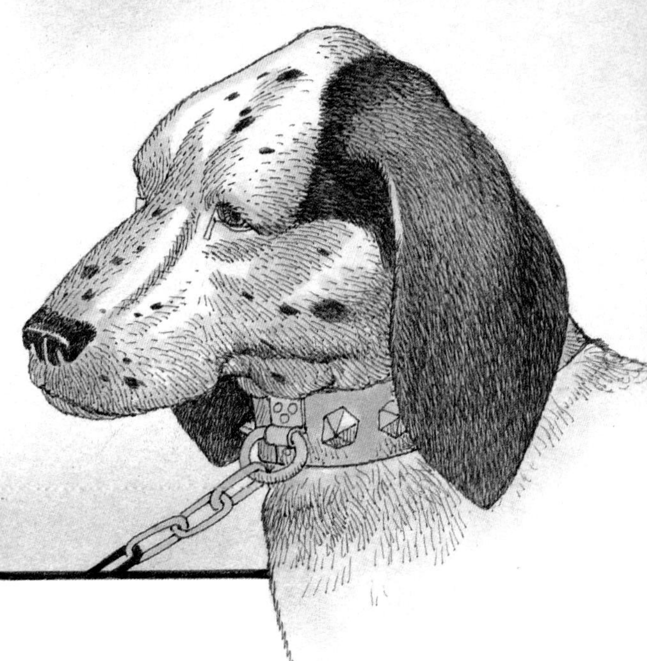

The Lark Knows When to Leave

A lark made her nest in the middle of a field of grain. It was a snug home in which to rear her young ones, well hidden from view among the stalks. The farmer came regularly to inspect his field and never knew that the lark and her family were living there.

When the wheat was tall and golden the farmer smiled with satisfaction. 'That's ready to cut,' he said. 'I'll get my neighbours to lend me a hand with it.'

The young larks flew to their mother and told her what the farmer had said. 'Let us get away while we can, mother,' they begged. 'This is no place for us. Our nest will be found when the corn is cut.'

'There is no need to leave yet,' their mother replied. 'If the farmer is relying on his neighbours to help him out, we have plenty of time.'

Some days later the farmer returned and saw that the corn was so ripe that the ears were shrivelling in the sun. 'I can't hang around waiting for other people,' he said. 'I'll hire some men and cut it myself.'

'Come, children,' said the mother lark. 'It's time to go.'

MORAL

If you want a job done, do it yourself.

How the Heron Was Paid

A wolf had a bone stuck in his throat. He went to a heron and said, 'Dear heron, be so kind as to put your head down my throat, and see if you can get this bone out.'

The heron was cautious. He did not fancy putting his head in the wolf's mouth. 'I charge a fee for that sort of thing,' he said.

'Of course, of course,' said the wolf. 'Just hurry up and take a look.' So the heron plunged his head down the wolf's throat and pulled out the bone.

But when he asked for his fee the wolf laughed. 'Count yourself lucky that I didn't bite your head off,' he said. 'That's payment enough.'

MORAL
Never trust those who live by preying upon others.

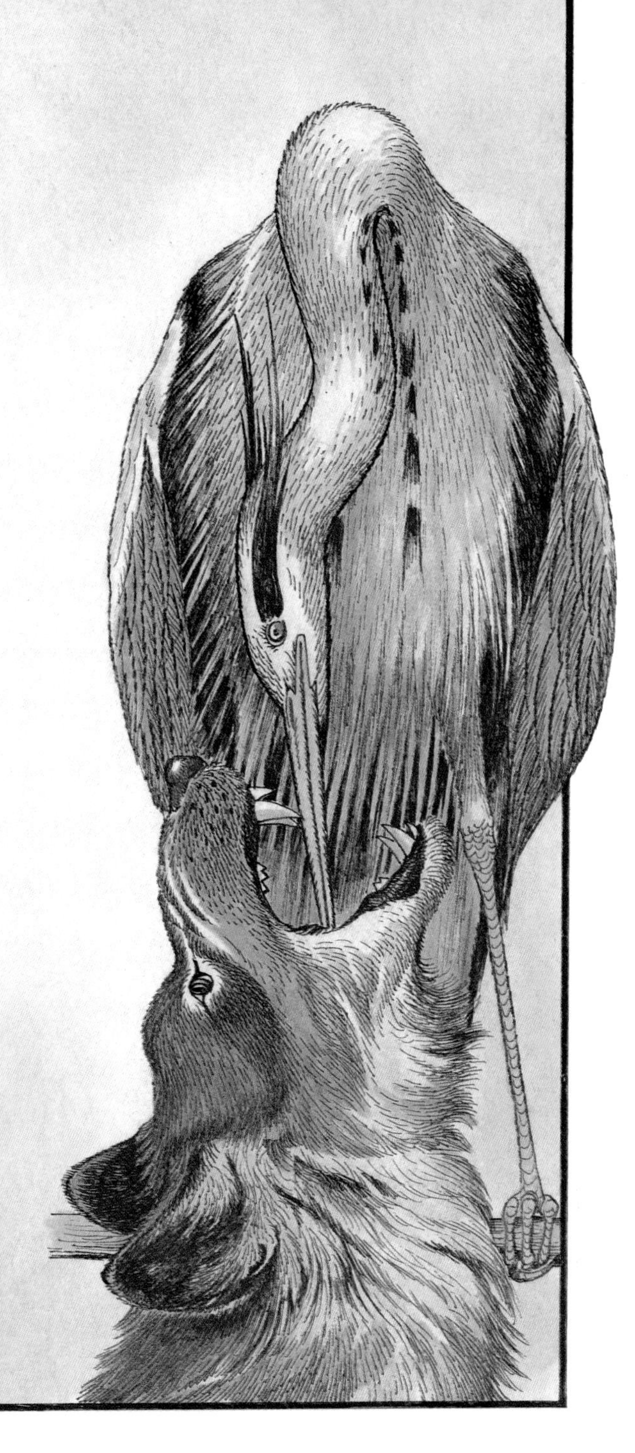

The Lion's Share

A lion and a wild ass formed a partnership to go hunting. The lion was very strong, but the wild ass could run faster, so joining forces seemed a good idea. Together they killed a large number of animals. The lion began the share-out. He divided the booty into three piles.

'As king of the animals, I am entitled to the first pile,' he announced. 'The second pile is mine, as my share in the partnership, and unless you want trouble, the third pile is mine too.'

Moral

Those in power make laws to suit themselves.

The Wolf Admires his Shadow

A wolf, prowling the hills at sunset, noticed how his shadow stretched at enormous length across the hillside in the sun's sinking light.

'How impressive I am,' he thought. 'I must be ten metres tall and twice as long. I shall not fear the lion any longer. Now that I know my strength he must make way for me.'

As the wolf stood gloating at the pleasing notion of lording it over all the other beasts, a lion leaped upon him and devoured him.

MORAL

Do not let conceit destroy your judgment.

The Grasshopper and the Ant

A grasshopper lived happily all summer, chirrupping in the sunshine, nodding and smiling to every creature he met, and without a care in the world. But when the cold weather came, he found that all the other creatures had already prepared nests or underground burrows, and filled them with food to last through the winter. The grasshopper had not thought to do this, and now he had no house and nothing to eat.

In despair the grasshopper went to his neighbour, the ant, and asked for the loan of a little something, a few morsels to keep him going until the spring. The ant looked disapproving. 'What were you doing all summer?' she asked. 'Didn't you think of stocking up for wintertime?'

'Never gave it a thought,' said the grasshopper. 'The sun was so lovely, I sang all day long.'

'You sang!' shrieked the outraged ant. 'Well, you can dancc now, for all I care.'

MORAL

Don't rely on good luck; plan for the future.

The Gnat on the Bull's Horns

A swarm of tiny gnats was hovering by a stream. A bull came down to the water to drink and a gnat settled on one of his horns.

'I hope you don't mind my sitting here,' said the gnat. 'If I'm too much of a weight, I can go on the willows over there.'

'You can go or stay,' said the bull. 'I hadn't noticed you were there.'

MORAL

When unimportant people put on airs, they make themselves ridiculous.

The Donkey that Fell in the Water

A pedlar, who bought and sold just about anything, was told that salt could be purchased very cheaply at the coast. So he went to the salt pans where sea water was dried, and bought as much salt as his donkey could carry.

On the way back, they were wading through a shallow stream when the donkey slipped and fell into the water. Most of the salt was dissolved and washed away, and when the donkey got up it found its load was much lighter. 'That's a tip worth knowing,' it thought. The next time the pedlar bought a load of salt, the donkey fell into the water on purpose and skipped home with less than half the load it started with.

But its master saw what it was up to. On the next trip he loaded the donkey as usual, and they set off home. Again the donkey fell into the water but this time, when it staggered up, its load was many times heavier than before. The pedlar had bought a load of sea sponges, which were now full of water.

MORAL

Don't try to be too clever; you may be caught out.

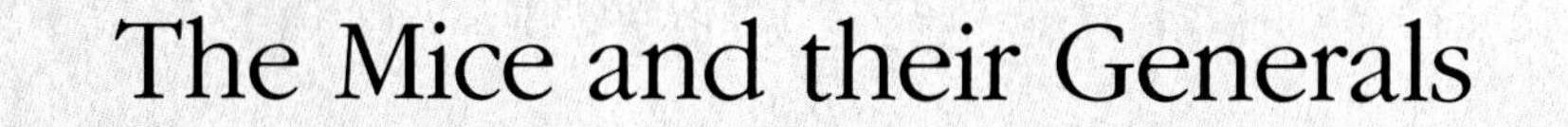

The Mice and their Generals

The mice were downhearted: in their continual war with the cats, they never had a victory. They met to discuss the matter, and decided that their defeats were due to lack of leadership. So they chose certain mice of noble birth and known courage to act as generals, train the troops and direct the battle.

When the cats next attacked, the mice marched out in orderly formation, led by the generals, who wore helmets of walnut shells as emblems of their rank. But still the mice were no match for the cats and were soon scattered. Most of them reached the safety of their holes, but the size of the shells strapped to the generals' heads prevented them from getting into theirs, and all the generals were caught and eaten.

MORAL
If you want a safe life, don't attempt to be a leader.

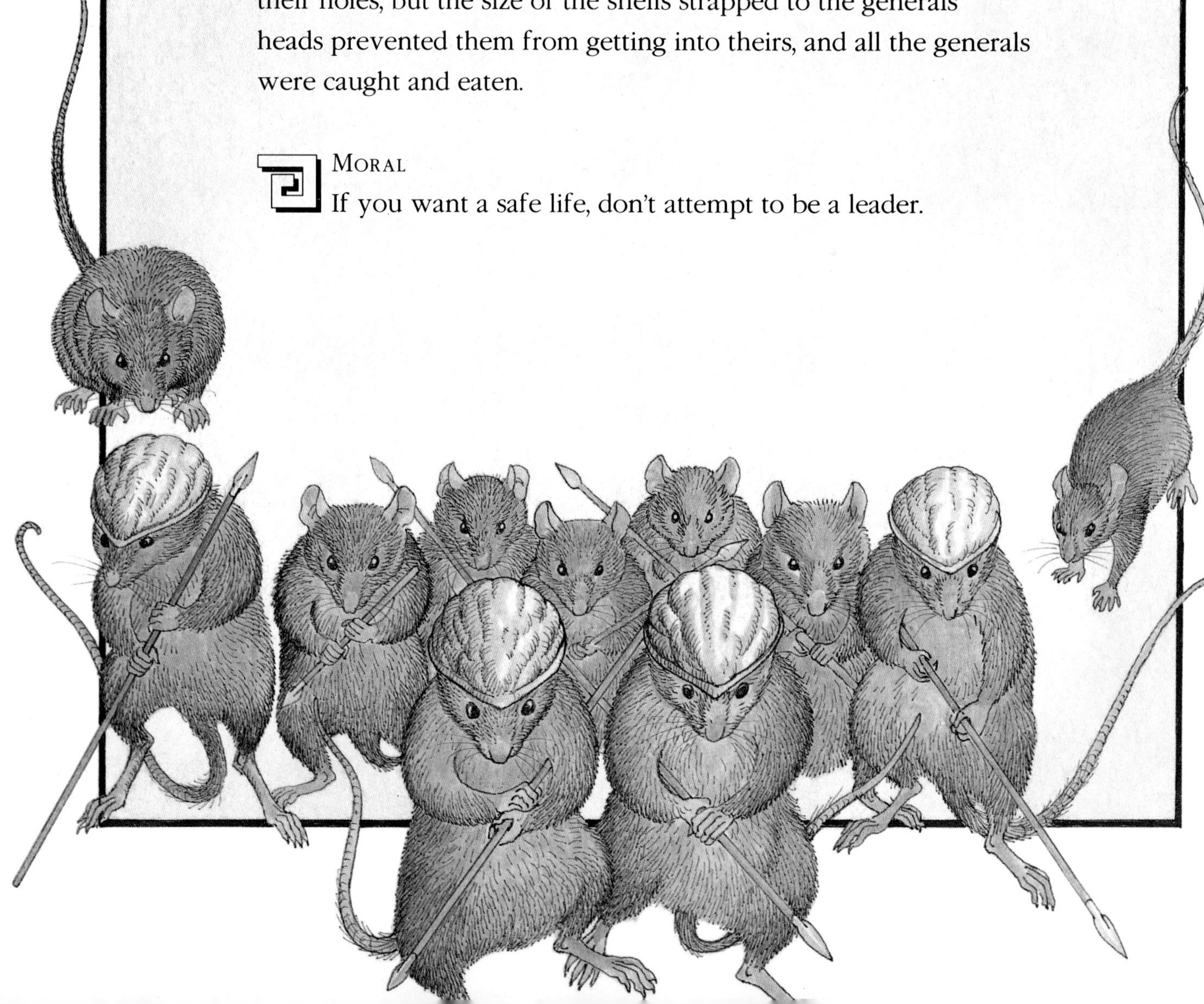

The Farmer and the Stork

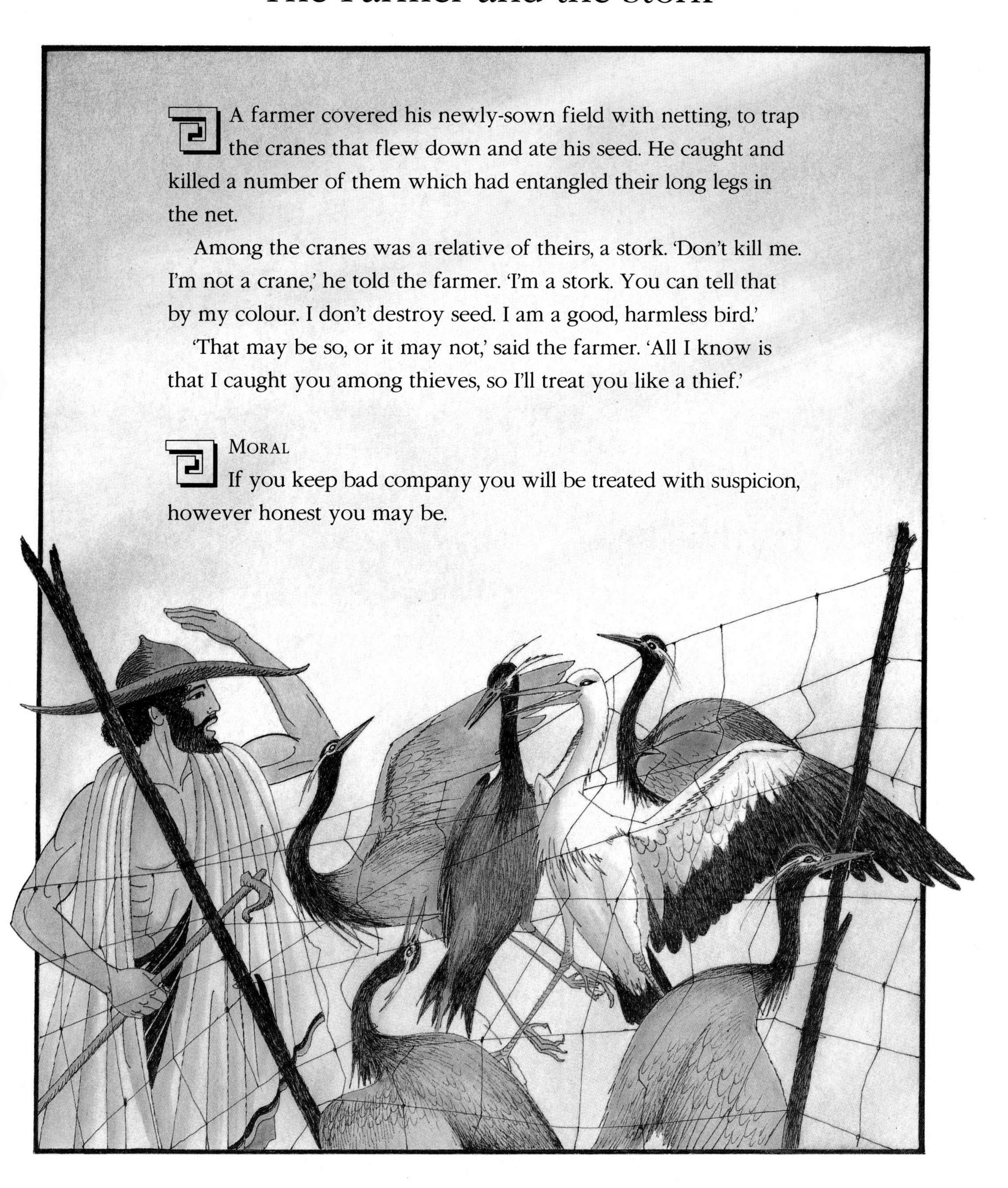

A farmer covered his newly-sown field with netting, to trap the cranes that flew down and ate his seed. He caught and killed a number of them which had entangled their long legs in the net.

Among the cranes was a relative of theirs, a stork. 'Don't kill me. I'm not a crane,' he told the farmer. 'I'm a stork. You can tell that by my colour. I don't destroy seed. I am a good, harmless bird.'

'That may be so, or it may not,' said the farmer. 'All I know is that I caught you among thieves, so I'll treat you like a thief.'

MORAL

If you keep bad company you will be treated with suspicion, however honest you may be.

The Lion and the Mouse

A lion caught a mouse and was about to eat it. 'Let me go,' begged the mouse. 'To swallow such a tiny morsel will make no difference to your hunger, but it will be a serious matter for me. If you spare me I will do you a favour in return.'

The haughty lion was so amused by this offer from a mouse that he lifted his paw and let it run away. Not long afterwards the lion ran into a net which hunters had set up to ensnare him. Though he struggled he could not free himself, and lay waiting to be killed. Then the mouse ran out of its hole and, gnawing through the net with its sharp teeth, set the lion free.

MORAL

Do not despise people who seem weak and insignificant. They may have something valuable to offer, in their own way.

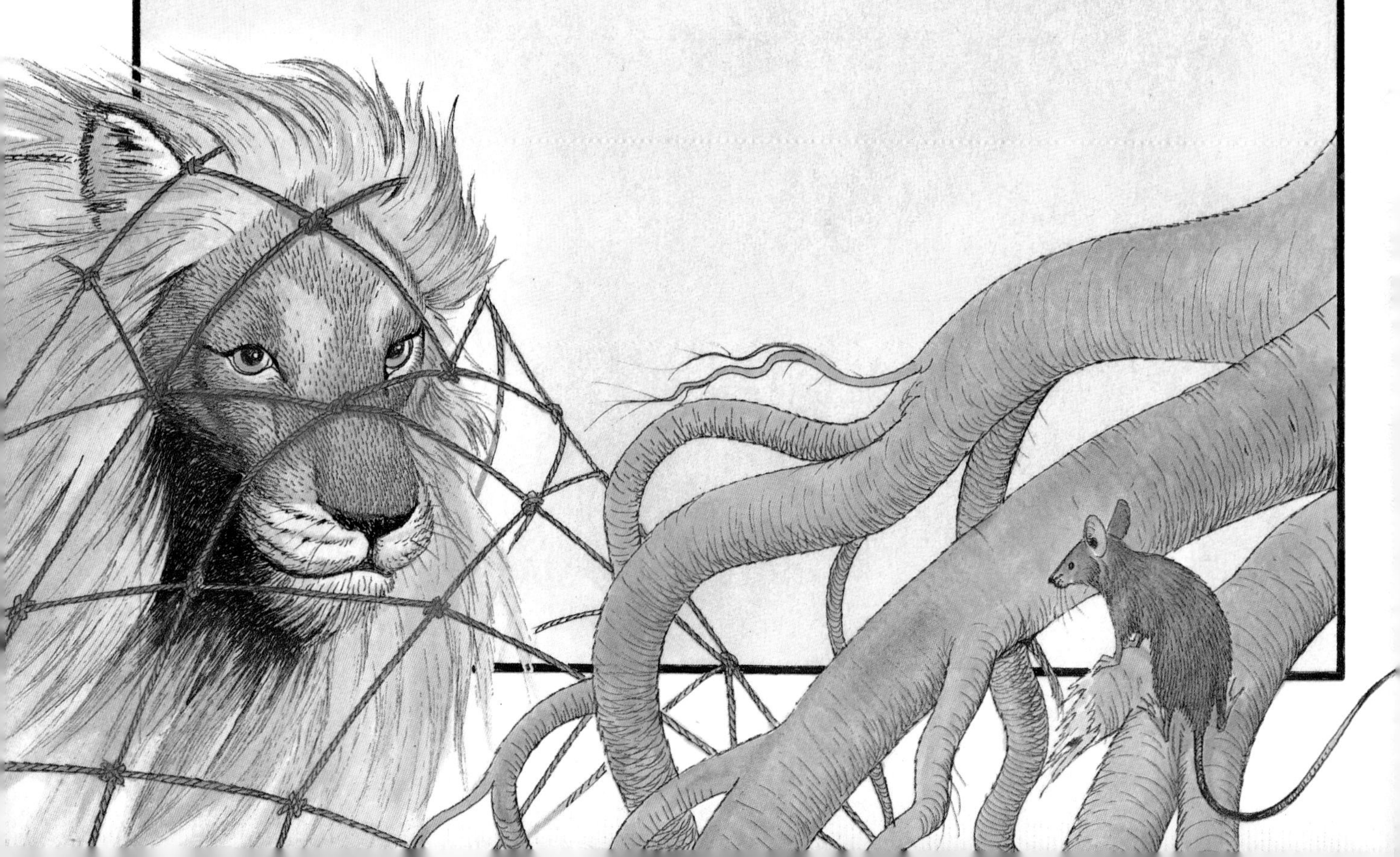

The Wolves and the Dogs

The wolves sent a deputation to the dogs who guarded the sheep. 'We have a proposal to put to you,' they said. 'It is foolish for us to be enemies, for we wolves and dogs are so alike that one could almost call us brothers. The only difference between us is that we are free while you are slaves. You work hard for your masters, but all you get from them is beatings and a few bones to eat. Let us join forces, take over the flocks and care for them together. We will share everything fairly between us, and eat whenever we want.'

The dogs were persuaded by this reasoning and let the wolves into the sheepfold; but the first thing the wolves did then was to kill the dogs.

MORAL
Treachery will be rewarded by treachery.

The Vixen and the Lioness

A vixen, who was the mother of a litter of bouncing cubs, had the temerity to boast to a lioness about her skills as a mother. She always had a large litter, she said, whereas the lioness only bore a single cub at a time.

'Only one,' was the reply, 'but a lion.'

MORAL

Quality is more important than quantity.

The Dog with the Bell

A farmer kept a number of dogs, one of which was a bad-tempered beast. It had a habit of coming up to people in a friendly way, wagging its tail between its legs, and then suddenly biting.

Its owner hung a bell around its neck, to warn everyone to keep out of its way. The dog imagined it had been especially honoured and pranced around the yard, shaking its neck to make the bell ring.

'What are you showing off for?' growled the oldest dog on the farm. 'That bell is not a reward. It's just a way of telling people about your nasty habits.'

MORAL
Ill-natured people do not realize how ugly their faults seem to others.

The Donkey Who Wanted to be Loved

A man had a donkey that he made to work hard, carrying heavy burdens and turning the mill that ground the flour. He also had a little dog that lived comfortably indoors. Whenever his master came home the dog rushed out to meet him, jumping up and down, wagging his tail, and pretending to bite him. The man laughed and joined in the game.

The donkey, watching, envied the dog. 'I work hard all day for the master,' he thought. 'Yet he never makes a fuss of me. That dog does nothing but eat and sleep and yet he is a favourite. It's my own fault. I've never gone out of my way to be liked. Yet I could easily play those tricks my master likes so much. In future I'll be cleverer.'

The next time his master came into the yard the donkey ran towards him, kicking up his heels and braying loudly. He planted his front hooves on his master's shoulders and began licking his face. The master, thinking he was being attacked, picked up a stick and beat the donkey unmercifully.

MORAL
Be realistic about yourself.

The Frogs Ask for a King

The frogs were discontented because, unlike most other creatures, they had no king to make laws and see that every frog was well-behaved. So they went to Zeus, King of the Gods, and asked to be given a king. Zeus laughed, and threw a huge log of wood into their pond.

At first the frogs were impressed by their new king, who was so large and floated in such majestic silence on the water, but soon they grew suspicious. They jumped on the log and inspected it. 'It is nothing but a lump of wood,' they croaked. 'Give us a real king.'

Then Zeus lost his temper and sent them a water snake which squirmed through the water, devouring the poor frogs one by one. In terror they went back to Zeus and begged to be saved from this king.

'You did not like what I sent you before,' the god replied. 'Now put up with what you have.'

MORAL

Don't complain about the way things are; the alternative may be much more unpleasant.

The Crow and the Water Jar

A thirsty crow discovered a large jar with a small amount of water at the bottom. He hopped on to the rim and dipped his beak inside, but found that he could not lean down far enough to drink. Then he tried to spill the water on the ground, but the jar was too heavy for him to tip.

He thought for a long time and then picked up a pebble and dropped it into the jar. He dropped in another pebble and then another, and each one made the level of the water rise a little, until he had dropped in so many that the water reached the top of the jar and he could drink.

MORAL

Reason solves difficult problems.

The Man Who Counted the Waves

A man stood on the seashore trying to count the waves. After counting many hundreds of them he lost count and was in despair because he had missed several waves. But a person approached him across the sand, who said that his name was Profit. 'Why trouble about the waves that have passed?' asked Profit. 'Forget them and begin counting from here.'

MORAL

Do not grieve over lost opportunities but make the most of those to come.

Borrowed Plumes

Zeus, King of the Gods, announced a competition to decide which of all the birds had the finest plumage. He himself would be the judge. The birds in great excitement began to get ready for the contest. They gathered at a pool to dip their feathers and comb their crests.

A dowdy old crow, who had no hope of winning, watched them as they preened themselves. Whenever one of them dropped a particularly pretty feather, the crow picked it up and stuck it in amongst his own, until he was entirely covered in borrowed plumes. Then he flew off to present himself to the King.

Zeus was about to give him the prize when the quick-witted swallow recognized her own little feather in the bunch. She swooped upon it and tweaked it out. Then all the other birds saw what a trick had been played on them and each flew up and seized its feather with an angry peck, until the crow was stripped of all his stolen finery. Then everyone could see what a dingy thing he really was.

MORAL

Don't boost your reputation by taking credit for other people's achievements. You will be found out in the end.

The Sleeping Dog and the Wolf

A dog was dozing in a farmyard when a wolf crept up and leaped upon him. The dog advised the wolf to let him go. 'You'd make a big mistake eating me now,' he said. 'You can see how thin and stringy I am. They only feed me on scraps. But next week my master's daughter is to be married. There'll be a big feast and all the juicy leftovers will be given to me. Come back and eat me then.'

'Very well,' said the wolf. 'I shall.' The following week he returned, and found the dog sunning himself on the roof of the barn. He called down to the wolf: 'Next time you want a meal, don't wait until the wedding.'

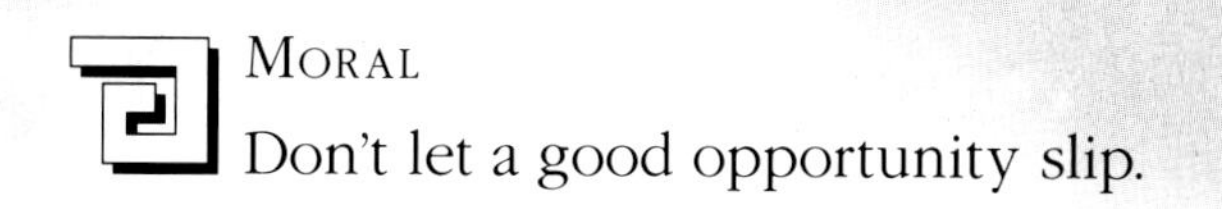

MORAL
Don't let a good opportunity slip.

The Soldier Who Destroyed his Weapons

A soldier, worn out by long years of service, discovered that he could no longer fight, for war had grown hateful to him. He vowed to give up soldiering and burn his weapons.

He made a fire and put the weapons on it, one by one. As he was bringing a trumpet to the flames it cried loudly that it was innocent of causing harm. 'I never struck a blow upon the battle-field,' it claimed. 'I only summoned men to fight, and I declare I made no very great noise about it.'

'Why, you deserve more punishment than any,' said the soldier, 'for without putting yourself in danger you urged the others to fight.' And he hurled the trumpet on to the fire.

MORAL

Those who stir up trouble are as much to blame as those who play an active part in it.

The Dog and her Puppies

A bitch who was about to have puppies asked another bitch if she could use her kennel to give birth in, for she had no shelter of her own. The second dog readily agreed.

But when, a little while later, she asked to have her kennel back, the new mother pleaded to be allowed to stay for a bit longer, just until her puppies were strong enough to leave home with her.

When that time too was up, the dog again demanded her kennel, more urgently. 'If you can get the better of me and all my offspring, you can have it,' was the answer she received.

Moral

Kindness is not always well repaid.

A more hard-headed interpretation would be: If you do a rash thing, watch out for the consequences.

or

Possession is nine-tenths of the law.

The Donkey and the Lyre

A donkey found a lyre on the grass. He had never seen such an object before and nuzzled it to discover whether it was good to eat. 'No good at all,' he decided, 'but it is a pretty thing all the same,' and he stroked the strings with his hoof.

The sweet sounds they gave forth filled his heart with pleasure and longing. 'There must be some art in this,' he thought. 'If I knew its secret I could make it sing. But I am, alas, a donkey in a field. Nobody would think of trying to teach that art to me.'

Moral

A talent cannot flourish in the wrong circumstances.

The Fox and the Stork

A fox invited a stork to dinner but offered her only a plate of soup. The fox lapped up his soup with ease and sniggered to see how the stork, who needed to plunge her beak deep in order to drink, got nothing.

Not long afterwards the stork asked the fox to dine with her. She put before him a long-necked jar full of food. 'Help yourself,' she said to her guest. The fox could not get even his nose into the jar, while the stork smiled and dipped in her beak.

Moral

Spiteful actions will be repaid in kind.

The Mule's Parents

A farmer had a mule* which he treated well. He did not make it work the whole day long, but let it have time to graze in a paddock.

The mule began to imagine itself a creature of importance. It raced around the paddock, tossing its neck about as if it had a long flowing mane, and calling out for all to hear: 'My mother was a horse! Watch me gallop. You can tell my mother was a horse.'

But then it stopped short and hung its head, for it had just remembered - its father was an ass!

MORAL

If you remember your bad qualities as well as your good ones you will not be tempted to boast.

**A mule is a cross between a horse and a donkey. It is a useful animal as it has some of the merits of a horse without its nervousness, and all the toughness of a donkey.*

The Frogs at the Well

In a long drought, when all the ponds were dry, some frogs in search of water came to a well. The first frog, already imagining its clammy depths, was just about to jump in.

'Wait,' said a second. 'It may be dried up like our pond, and once in you will not be able to get out again. Let's look before we leap.'

MORAL

Pause to think before you act.

The Wolf and the Lamb

A wolf and a lamb came to a stream to drink. The lamb took care to keep well clear of the wolf and went to a part of the bank lower down the stream. The wolf saw him and longed to sink his teeth into him. Looking for an excuse, he declared that the lamb was muddying his drinking water.

'How can I be?' said the lamb. 'The water flows downstream from you to me.'

'Never mind that,' said the wolf. 'You're a liar. I know you spread those slanders about me six months ago.'

'Why, six months ago I wasn't even born,' protested the lamb.

'Well, if it wasn't you, it was your father,' said the wolf, and tore him to pieces.

MORAL

The strong will always find reasons for oppressing the weak.

The Goatherd and the Wild Goats

A goatherd, caught in a snowstorm on the hills, decided to shelter his animals in a cave for the night. The goats were hungry, for they had found nothing to nibble in the frozen ground, so the goatherd tore down leafy branches which he carried into the cave for his animals to eat.

Once inside, he discovered that a herd of wild goats had already taken refuge there. They were bigger, fatter animals than his, and there were more of them. 'If these were mine too,' he thought, 'I would have a better herd than any man I know.' So he fed the leaves to the wild goats in the hope of taming them, and lay down to sleep.

When he woke the next morning the wild goats were gone, and his own were dead from cold and starvation.

MORAL
Be satisfied with what you have.

The Horse and the Donkey

A man kept a fine horse for show, and a donkey to carry burdens. The horse used to prance along while the old donkey staggered behind, weighted by his load.

'Please help,' the donkey begged the horse. 'If you took some of this load I could manage, but like this I can't last much longer.'

'Don't bother me,' replied the horse.

The donkey plodded on for a while, stumbled, and fell dead. The man at once began to skin him, for his hide would be useful. Then he put the donkey's burden on the horse and threw the donkey skin on top.

How sorry the horse was then that he had not helped the donkey! For his load was now much heavier than it would have been if he had shared with his companion.

MORAL
Help other people in their troubles. You may need help in return.

The Travellers and the Bear

Two men set out on a journey. Their path was rough and dangerous, over wild hillsides and through forests in which savage beasts lurked, but they were not as afraid as they might have been, for they had agreed to help each other in every peril.

As they were following a narrow wooded track, a she-bear rushed upon them. One man fled towards an over-hanging oak and pulled himself to safety in its branches. The second had no time to move and threw himself on the ground. He lay as if he were dead, for he had heard that bears will never touch dead meat. The bear sniffed all

around him, rolling his head over with her paw and snuffling in his ear. Finally she shambled off into the trees.

The first man then dropped down from his perch and asked his companion jokingly what the bear had been whispering in his ear. 'She gave me some good advice,' said the second man. 'She warned me to steer clear of situations where the only help was from the likes of you.'

MORAL

In times of trouble, we learn to tell false friends from true.

The Dog, the Donkey, and the Letter

A donkey and a dog were walking along together when they came across a letter lying in the road.

The donkey picked it up and began reading it out to the dog. It was about animal feed - grasses, hay, and oats.

The dog got impatient. 'Skip that bit,' he said. 'See if it has anything to say about meat and bones.'

The donkey read out the whole letter but meat and bones were never mentioned.

'Throw it away,' said the dog. 'It's absolute rubbish.'

MORAL

Few people are interested in anything but their own concerns.

The Oak and the Reeds

A tall oak grew on a mountainside. It was a giant among trees, with a massive trunk, and leaves that darkened the sky. But a great wind tore the oak from the ground by its roots and hurled it into the river. As the oak was swept along, it saw the reeds along the river bank swaying in the gale.

'How do those frail reeds withstand the wind, whilst I, a mighty oak, could not?' it wondered.

'You fought the wind,' the reeds replied. 'We bend our necks and let it pass over us.'

MORAL

It is dangerous to play a grand role in life. If you oppose people more powerful than yourself they may destroy you. But they ignore the meek and the obedient.

The Wild Boar and the Fox

A wild boar was standing by a tree, sharpening his tusks by rubbing them against the tree trunk. A fox, who liked to express an opinion on things that did not concern him, remarked that this was an odd way to spend the time; the boar had no need to sharpen his tusks as there was not the slightest danger anywhere in sight.

'When I see danger there will be no time to sharpen my tusks,' said the boar. 'Yet they will be ready.'

MORAL
Be prepared.

The Wolf in Sheep's Clothing

A wolf thought of a cunning way to help himself to as many sheep as he wanted. He covered himself with a sheepskin and trotted in among the sheep, pretending to nibble the grass here and there as he went. When the shepherd rounded up the flock at dusk and drove it into the sheepfold, the wolf was driven in with the rest.

But the wily beast soon had reason to regret his cleverness. The shepherd took out a long knife and, wanting a good joint of mutton for his supper, seized the nearest animal which happened to be the wolf, and killed it.

MORAL

You can be undone by your own devices.

The Wolf Entertains

A young kid lagged behind the other goats and was caught by a wolf. 'I can see that you mean to make an end of me,' said the kid to the wolf, 'but if I am to be your supper let us prepare the meal in style. If you will play upon the flute I shall dance for you before you dine.' So the wolf piped and the kid danced and the noise attracted the farm dogs, who rushed upon the wolf and drove him off.

'I have only myself to blame,' the wolf growled as he slunk away. 'My job is being a butcher. It was foolish to try to be a musician as well.'

MORAL

If you want to succeed, stick to what you do well.

The Dog with the Bigger Bone

A dog snatched a bone from a butcher's shop and ran off with it in his mouth. The bone was red and meaty, and the dog felt very pleased with himself.

As he crossed a narrow bridge he saw in the water what seemed to be another dog, with a bone which he felt sure was bigger and juicier than his own. He wanted that one too, so he made a snap at his reflection in the stream. As he opened his mouth the bone fell from his jaws and was lost in the water.

MORAL

By being too greedy you may lose what you have.

The Eagle Whose Wings were Clipped

A man captured an eagle and clipped its wings to prevent it flying. He thought it would be amusing to keep it in a cage, which he set up in the yard beside the hen coops. Sometimes he let the eagle out, to flap about the yard as the hens did. The king of birds could not endure the shame of living like a barnyard fowl. It would not eat, and waited to die.

An acquaintance of the eagle's owner pitied the bird and bought it from him for a large sum. He rubbed its feathers with myrrh* to help them sprout, and when they were fully grown he let the eagle fly away.

To show its gratitude the eagle returned with a present in its beak - a rabbit for the man's supper, the best that it could find. 'That was a wasted gift,' observed a fox sardonically. 'Why give it to someone who is already your friend? You should have given it to the other man. It would have counted in your favour if ever you were to fall into his hands again.'

MORAL

Only the mean-spirited count the cost of doing good or the benefits it may bring them.

**Myrrh is the scented resin of a tree found in Turkey and Greece. An extract from it was used medicinally, though whether it would have helped birds' feathers to grow is hard to say.*

The Sick Hen

A hen was feeling very ill. A cat heard that she was sick and hurried to visit her. 'How are you?' she asked. 'Can I do anything for you? I am so interested in your health. Do you think you will get better?'

'If you go away,' replied the hen, 'I'm sure I will.'

MORAL

When your enemies are friendly, you may be sure they mean to gain by it.

The Shipwrecked Man

A ship, caught in a storm, was sinking rapidly. Everyone on board leaped off and started swimming for the shore, except for one rich man from Athens. He did nothing but pray loudly to Athena, the goddess of his native city, to send him help, promising her rich offerings if she would save him.

But his companions shouted from the water: 'Don't wait for Athena. Start swimming!'

MORAL

Don't expect other people to get you out of difficulties. Cope with them yourself.

The Old Lion

A lion found that he was getting too old to catch his prey. He was short of breath and his legs were too stiff. So he lay down in a cave and pretended to be very ill. The other animals heard his feeble groans and felt sorry for him. The more tender-hearted thought they should offer help. As one by one they came to visit him in his den, the lion scooped them up and ate them, with no trouble at all. In this way he lived comfortably.

One day a fox came to the mouth of the cave and enquired, most politely, whether the king of beasts was feeling better. 'Don't stand out there, dearest fox,' said the lion. 'Come in and tell me the news. I hear no gossip, lying here alone.'

'Your majesty must excuse me,' replied the fox. 'I notice something which has sent all the news right out of my head. Amongst all the animal tracks leading into your cave, I don't see a single one coming out again.'

MORAL

Keep your eyes open and avoid other people's mistakes.

The Stag at the Pool

A young stag went to a pool to drink. As he bent his head to the water he caught sight of his reflection in the pool. His branching antlers filled him with pride and satisfaction, but his legs seemed poor in comparison, spindly and frail. He felt ashamed of them.

Just then the sound of barking hounds warned him that huntsmen were on his trail. He bounded off so fast that he would soon have left them behind, if he had not run into the wood. Here his antlers became entangled in the branches and he was easily caught.

'How wrong I was,' he thought. 'My legs, which I despised, would have carried me to safety, but my antlers have betrayed me.'

MORAL

We often make bad judgments because we do not recognize the true value of things.

The Downtrodden Snake

A snake lamented that people lost no opportunity to stamp it underfoot. It complained to Zeus, King of the Gods, about the treatment it received.

'If you had bitten the first person who trod on you,' the god replied, 'no one else would have dared to put a foot near you.'

MORAL
We respect those whom we fear.

The Farmer's Bequest to his Sons

An old farmer on his death bed told his sons that a treasure lay buried in his vineyard.

When he had died the sons began eagerly to look for this fortune. Though they dug every inch of the vineyard they found nothing, but the vines were grateful for this good digging. They grew thick and strong, with so many fat grapes that the sons' profit was greater than in any previous year.

MORAL

Hard work brings its own reward.

The Clown and the Countryman

A countryman came to town and found it thronged with entertainers who were competing daily for a prize. The judging was done by the audience: the act that it cheered loudest was the winner.

The countryman joined the crowd to watch a clown who came on stage wrapped in a cloak from which amazing squeals and grunts were heard. 'You've got a pig in there. Show us the pig!' called the crowd. The clown threw open his cloak but it was empty. He had made the sounds himself. The crowd whistled and stamped and declared that nothing could have been more like a pig. At that the countryman stepped forward and swore he could do better. 'Tomorrow,' he promised, 'we'll have a match.'

Next day a huge crowd gathered for 'the battle of the pigs'.

No one believed the clown could be beaten and he was cheered louder than ever. Then the countryman appeared, also wrapped in a cloak. In fact he had a pig underneath, and by giving it a few tweaks he produced some very piggy noises. The people laughed. 'That's not much like a pig,' they said. 'The other was far better.' Then the countryman produced the pig, proving to them what poor judges they had been.

MORAL
The majority can often be wrong.
or
Art is truer than life.

The Crab and her Daughter

'Walk straight,' said a mother crab to her daughter. 'You are always shuffling sideways. Nothing looks worse. It makes such a bad impression.'

'I am sorry, mother dear,' said her daughter. 'But what am I to do when I have only your example to follow?'

MORAL

Don't tell other people how to behave unless you are perfect yourself.

The Hares Take Comfort

The hares were so miserable that they decided to kill themselves. 'We are such weak creatures,' they said. 'Everyone despises us. There is nothing we are good at but running away.'

They rushed to the river bank to hurl themselves into the water; but their approach terrified some frogs who leaped away into the reeds.

'Turn back,' called the hares to each other. 'These creatures are more timid than we are. Let's forget this idea and go home.'

MORAL

When you think of other people's troubles, your own may not seem so bad.

The Nightingale and the Bat

A nightingale in a cage, hanging at an open window, began to sing when darkness fell. A bat skimming past outside paused to inquire why she waited until night to sing, and was silent during the day.

'Singing in the daylight is dangerous,' the nightingale replied. 'I was captured doing that.'

'Then you should have taken the precaution before you were caught,' said the bat. 'It's pointless now.'

MORAL

It's easy to be wise after the event.

A Guide to Aesop's Beasts

Index of Themes

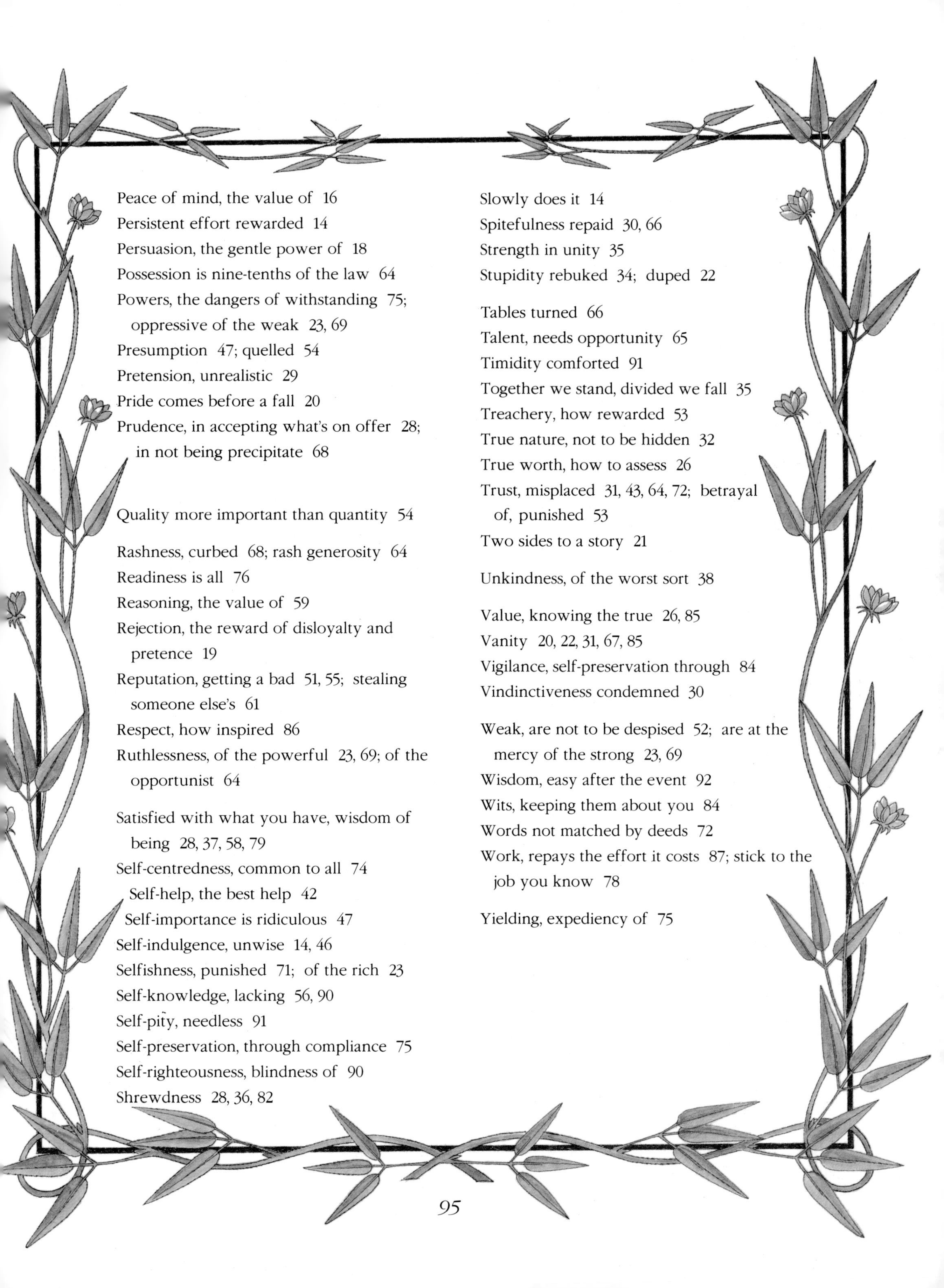